Mr Teach-bot and the Bionic Board

Story by Cameron Macintosh

Illustrations by Gustavo Mazali

Contents

Chapter 1

A New Invention

It had been a busy morning for Hugo, his friend Jasmine and the other students in class 4T. Their day had started with a hoverboard safety class, followed by a robot-repair lesson.

Their teacher, Mr Teach-bot, was very good at robot repairs … because he happened to be a robot himself! Mr Teach-bot also liked to invent things.

Just after lunch, Mr Teach-bot announced to the class that he had been working on a new invention in his spare time.

"Oh, no," whispered Hugo to Jasmine. "I hope the new invention is better than the electric pencil sharpener he made. It completely gobbled up my pencil."

"And I hope it's better than the electric stapler he invented," replied Jasmine. "It stapled itself shut and never worked again!"

"This screen doesn't work very well any more," said Mr Teach-bot. "I've made something much, much better! I'll bring it in tomorrow."

Jasmine and Hugo looked at each other, grinning.

"Tomorrow is going to be a very interesting day," whispered Jasmine.

Chapter 2

Meet the Bionic Board

The next morning, Mr Teach-bot stood by the classroom door. "Are you all ready to see my new invention?" he asked.

"Yes!" everyone replied.

Mr Teach-bot opened the door, and wheeled a strange-looking device into the classroom.

"Please say hello to my new assistant, the Bionic Board!"

The board had a pair of long, bendy arms, with an eyeball at the end of each one.

"This board can do all sorts of useful things," said Mr Teach-bot. "With those arms and eyes, it can keep watch on everything happening in the classroom. If any of you are having trouble with your schoolwork, it will let me know immediately. What's more, it can answer any question you want to ask it."

Mr Teach-bot switched the board on. Its screen lit up brightly and its arms waved around in circles.

"Hello, Bionic Board," Mr Teach-bot said. "What is the capital city of France?"

"Paris, of course," replied the board.

"And what is the name on the clock up there?"

The board lifted one of its arms all the way up to the clock on the wall and looked at it with a large eye.

"The name is Gribble," it replied. "This clock was made by Jessica Gribble in the year 2035."

Jasmine and Hugo were very impressed. They were not used to seeing Mr Teach-bot's inventions work so well!

Chapter 3

Strange Ideas

That afternoon, the Bionic Board helped Mr Teach-bot in class. As the students worked, the board looked over their shoulders with its eyeball arms to check how they were going. It gave Hugo quite a fright while he was trying to do some quiet reading!

In the middle of the lesson, Mr Teach-bot suddenly said, “My battery is running low. I must do a quick recharge.”

“Don’t worry,” he added, stepping towards the doorway, “the Bionic Board will take care of everything while I’m gone.”

"Today, we are going to learn all about carrots," said the Bionic Board. "A carrot is a bright blue vegetable. It is very sweet and is often eaten for dessert."

The students looked at each other in confusion.

"Are you quite sure about that?" asked Hugo.

"I am completely sure," replied the Bionic Board.

When Mr Teach-bot returned a few minutes later, Hugo told him that the board seemed to have strange ideas about carrots.

"I'm sure the board is fine, Hugo," said Mr Teach-bot. "I know I haven't had a lot of luck with my inventions, but this one is a great success. Let's get back to our lesson."

Chapter 4

The Spelling Task

The next day, Mr Teach-bot was about to give the class a spelling task when he suddenly felt tired.

"Sorry, class," he said. "I need to go and recharge again. The Bionic Board will give you the spelling task."

When Mr Teach-bot left the room, the Bionic Board lit up brightly. "Please write down these words," it said, and it began to read out a list of 20 words. "Urgent, spanner, angrily ..."

The students typed the words into their tablets, then sent them to the Bionic Board. The board went quiet as everyone's results flashed onto its screen.

The board threw its arms up into the air. "You have all done very poorly," it said.

Hugo, Jasmine and the other students looked at each other. "How is this possible?" they asked.

Just then, Mr Teach-bot returned to the classroom and looked at the Bionic Board's screen.

"Goodness me," he said. "These results are very disappointing. I will have to tell your parents that you all need extra help with your spelling."

“I don’t think we could have all done as badly as the Bionic Board says,” replied Hugo.

“The Bionic Board knows what it’s doing,” said Mr Teach-bot. “You will just have to work harder to improve your spelling!”

The next morning, several parents came to class at the start of the first lesson.

"I'm very concerned about yesterday's spelling task," said Hugo's mum. "Hugo has always been good at spelling!"

Mr Teach-bot had a close look at what the students had written the previous day.

"Oh, no!" he said. "My new invention has made a very big mistake. Instead of doing badly like the board said, nearly everyone scored 20 out of 20. I will take my invention home and fix it so nothing like this can happen again."

Chapter 5

Back-to-Front Facts!

The next day, Mr Teach-bot brought the Bionic Board back to class. He was so sure it was now running perfectly that he asked it to supervise a maths test.

The Bionic Board displayed the sums on its screen and the students answered them on their tablets.

At the end of the test, the board said that no one had done the sums correctly.

Everyone was quite upset, but Jasmine stood up and spoke. "I can see a pattern," she said. "This board only seems to like wrong answers."

"What do you mean?" asked Mr Teach-bot.

"Let me give you a demonstration," replied Jasmine. "Bionic Board, what colour is a seagull?"

"Black," said the board.

"And where do fish live?"

"On the land," it replied.

"Goodness me," said Mr Teach-bot. "You are right. I have made another invention that has failed."

"Don't feel bad," said Hugo. "Your board will be very useful. If it says we're right, we'll know we're wrong, and if it says we're wrong, we'll know we're right!"

"What do you mean?" asked Mr Teach-bot.

"Listen to this!" replied Jasmine. "Is an elephant big?" she asked the board.

"No, an elephant is very small," it said.

Everyone laughed.

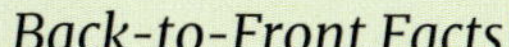

"Is January the first month of the year?" Hugo asked the board.

"No," it replied. "December is the first month."

The children were soon using the board to answer all sorts of questions, in a back-to-front way. It was very helpful – especially when the students needed to make sure that an answer was wrong!

“Gosh,” said Mr Teach-bot. “This isn’t quite what I was hoping my invention would do, but if it’s helping my students, then I’m happy, too!”